S0-DZF-359

The Star Who Almost Wasn't There

For the children of
Mattie Anne Free Methodist Church,
I hope you love this story
and the little star. Please
share it with your
friends.

Hahn
2014

Copyright © 2013 Pamela Hahn

All rights reserved. No part of this book may be used or reproduced by any means,
graphic, electronic, or mechanical, including photocopying, recording, taping or by any
information storage retrieval system without the written permission of the publisher
except in the case of brief quotations embodied in critical articles and reviews.

WestBow Press books may be ordered through booksellers or by contacting:

WestBow Press
A Division of Thomas Nelson
1663 Liberty Drive
Bloomington, IN 47403
www.westbowpress.com
1-(866) 928-1240

Because of the dynamic nature of the Internet, any web addresses or links contained in
this book may have changed since publication and may no longer be valid. The views
expressed in this work are solely those of the author and do not necessarily reflect the views
of the publisher, and the publisher hereby disclaims any responsibility for them.

Any people depicted in stock imagery provided by Thinkstock are models,
and such images are being used for illustrative purposes only.
Certain stock imagery © Thinkstock.

ISBN: 978-1-4497-6915-4 (sc)
ISBN: 978-1-4497-6916-1 (e)

Library of Congress Control Number: 2012918549

Printed in the United States by Bookmasters, Inc
30 Amberwood Parkway
Ashland OH 44805
September 2013
M11294

WestBow Press rev. date: 9/3/2013

WESTBOW
PRESS
A DIVISION OF THOMAS NELSON

The Star Who Almost Wasn't There

A Story of the First Christmas
For Stacey Ruth Hahn
And all little children everywhere

PAMELA HAHN

It happened once upon a time
Two thousand years and more ago.

A tiny star lived in the sky,

a tiny star who could not glow.

A **star** so dim, a **star** so small
that no one noticed him at all.

jesse

He was alone in the sky above,
for there was no child for him to love.

Each other star has a child somewhere:
a child to love, for whom to care,

a child to make wishes
by evening starlight,

a child to be watched
over late at night.

But the little star had no one.

Is it any wonder, though,
for the tiny star could scarce be seen
because he could not glow.

Every night the tiny star
would sail across the sky above
and search the earth both near and far
to find a child for him to love.

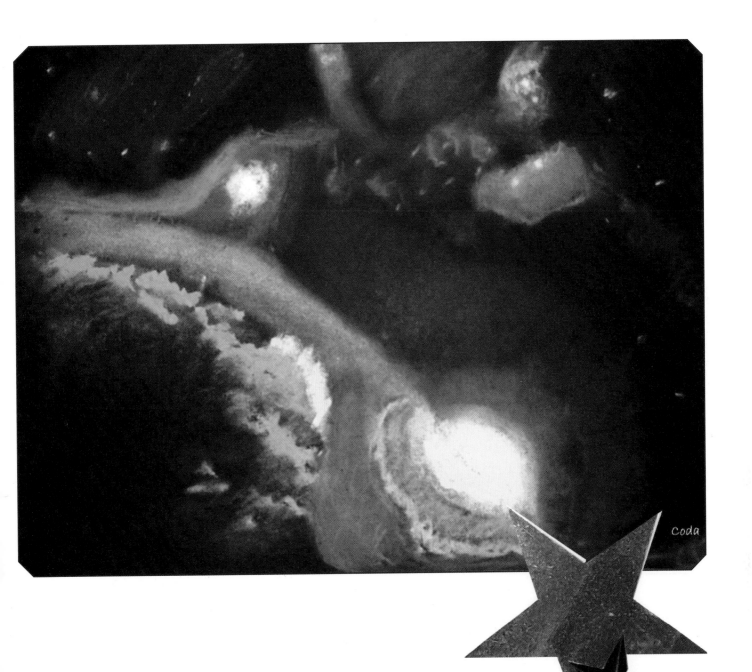

coda

**But though he traveled far and wide,
no child could he find anywhere
who'd give love to a tiny star,
a star who almost wasn't there.**

Then one night the star **dipped down over a dark and peaceful town where in a stable's manger lay a newborn babe atop the hay.**

Lauren

And there the child so peacefully slept
that the tiny star broke down and wept.
His tears awoke the child from sleep,
and the Christ child saw the small star weep.

The **star** began to sail on by,

but he had caught the Christ child's eye.

A smile spread over the young babe's face,
and the world was filled with holy grace.

Then the child reached out his hand
as if to touch the star **above,**
to let him know that he'd been seen
and let him know that he was loved.

The star knew then, in all the lands
that he had traveled, near and far,
there was no other child like this:
a child who would love a tiny star.

The star's heart began to fill with joy
and he began to glow,

he was brighter than any
star had ever been,
for he glowed with the light
that comes from within.

Filled with joy and shining bright,

he rose high into the sky above

to proclaim unto the whole wide world

the wonderful gift of the Christ child's love.

Teara

He called to the angels in heaven above
and told them of the Lord's great love.

Then they flew down amidst the stars bright rays to sing to the Lord their songs of praise.

**To shepherds in the fields afar,
great light was sent by the little star.
An angel also went to them
to tell of the child born in Bethlehem.**

Far to the east, where the sun does rise,
lived three men, old and wise,
who saw the star's radiant light
and let it guide them through the night.

**Then to the stable in Bethlehem
came the shepherds and three wise kings**

**bearing gifts for God's new son
while angels did around him sing.**

The whole world heard the news that night
brought to them by the bright starlight.
Each bowed his head in prayer and then
gave thanks to God for his love of men.

The tiny star bowed his head too
and made a vow that very night:
"I will love the Lord, my God,
with all my heart,
and all my soul,
and all my *light*."

The End

Contributors to the artwork:

Lauren Michelle Emmett

Onteara 'Teara' Rain Smaga

William Coda Emmett

Jose Robert Emmett

Jesse Michael Emmett

Jayante 'Jay' Daniel Jordan

Sarah Heavenly Lancaster

Caulier Michael Lancaster

Kathrynn Kay Emmett

Willow Orion Emmett

Jakob Alexander Emmett